# Lulu Bell and the Circus Pup

A Random House book
Published by Random House Australia Pty Ltd
Level 3, 100 Pacific Highway, North Sydney NSW 2060
www.randomhouse.com.au

First published by Random House Australia in 2014
Copyright © Belinda Murrell 2014
Illustrations copyright © Serena Geddes 2014

Addresses for companies within the Random House Group can be found at
www.randomhouse.com.au/offices

National Library of Australia
Cataloguing-in-Publication Entry

Author: Murrell, Belinda
Title: Lulu Bell and the circus pup/Belinda Murrell; illustrated by Serena Geddes
ISBN: 978 0 85798 199 8 (paperback)
Series: Murrell, Belinda. Lulu Bell; 5
Target audience: For primary school age
Subjects:  Circus – Juvenile fiction
           Dogs – Juvenile fiction
Other authors/contributors: Geddes, Serena
Dewey number: A823.4

Cover and internal illustrations by Serena Geddes
Cover design by Christabella Designs
Internal design and typesetting in 16/22 pt Bembo by Ingo Voss, based on series
design by Anna Warren, Warren Ventures
Printed in Australia by Griffin Press, an accredited ISO AS/NZS 14001:2004
Environmental Management System printer

Random House Australia uses papers that are natural, renewable and recyclable
products and made from wood grown in sustainable forests. The logging and
manufacturing processes are expected to conform to the environmental regulations
of the country of origin.

# Lulu Bell and the Circus Pup

Belinda Murrell

Illustrated by Serena Geddes

RANDOM HOUSE AUSTRALIA

Molly       Lulu       Dad

Mum　　Gus　　Rosie

For Jessica, who inspired me to write about a circus pup. And to the cast and crew of *Cavalia*, especially Eric and Mathieu, and Katie and Fairland – fearless riders extraordinaire, who all generously shared their passion for horses and performing. You are amazing!

# Chapter 1

# Gymnastics

It was Tuesday afternoon after school. Lulu Bell and her sister Rosie were at gymnastics class. There were seven girls and six boys, and they were all practising their cartwheels.

Lulu swung sideways from her feet to her hands and over again. She did twenty cartwheels in a row. Her best record yet. On the last one she wobbled but landed safely on her feet.

'Beautiful cartwheels, Lulu,' said Miss Carolina. 'I like the way you are keeping your legs nice and straight.'

Lulu felt a glow of pride. 'Thanks, Miss Carolina. I've been practising every day in the garden at home.'

Mum sat watching with the other mothers. Lulu's little brother Gus was doing forward rolls with his friends. He was too young to do classes yet, but he liked to copy his older sisters. The only problem was that he refused to take off his cowboy hat and boots. This made it hard to roll in a straight line.

The last part of the class was walking on the balance beam. Lulu concentrated hard, and held her arms out to the side. She felt like a tightrope walker. Lulu loved doing gymnastics.

'Okay, gang,' said Miss Carolina. 'Great work. I'll see you all next Tuesday. Keep practising!'

'Goodbye, Miss Carolina,' chorused the children. 'See you next week.'

The kids milled around, chatting and laughing. Lulu's friend Jessica skipped over. Her twin brothers Jack and Toby were great friends with Gus.

'Have you heard the news, Lulu?' asked Jessica. 'The circus is coming to Shelly Beach. Mum said we can go on Friday night.'

'The circus?' said Lulu. Her eyes shone with excitement. 'We went to the

3

circus when it came two years ago.
It was fantastic.'

'Will they have lions and elephants
and monkeys?' asked Rosie.

'There's a poster on the noticeboard,'
said Jessica. 'Let's take a look.'

The children crowded around the
noticeboard. The poster showed a clown
with a white-painted face, a smiling red
mouth, a huge red nose and a curly blue
wig.

'Starlight Circus,' read Lulu. 'A
dazzling show with acrobats, jugglers
and crazy clowns.'

'Starring camels, horses and
performing dogs,' added Rosie.

Mum came over to join them.
'Time to head home, honey buns.'

'Look, Mum,' said Lulu. 'The circus
is coming. Can we go? Pleeease?'

'Pretty please with cherries on top?'
said Rosie.

Mum read the poster and smiled.
'We'll see. Come on.'

The three Bell children called
goodbye to their friends. The girls slipped
their school uniforms over their blue
leotards. Rosie also pulled on her angel
wings. Gus climbed into the pram.

Outside, the family dogs Asha and Jessie were tied up in the shade of a tree. They jumped up and wriggled with excitement to see the children.

'Good girls. Did you miss us?' Lulu asked. She untied the dogs' leads.

'Woof,' said Asha. Jessie smiled her big doggy smile.

'You know, I think we might walk home the long way today,' said Mum. 'It would be a nice change to walk back through Lagoon Park.'

Lulu turned around. 'The long way?' she asked. 'Why?'

Mum had a cheeky smile on her face. 'Oh, who knows what fabulous sights we might see if we go the long way?'

*Mmmm*, thought Lulu. *Mum's up to something. I wonder what it could be?*

## Chapter 2

# Lagoon Park

Lagoon Park was a long, narrow stretch of grass beside a wide lagoon. The late afternoon sun glinted on the water. Wispy rushes fringed the banks. Fat brown ducks waddled on the shore.

Gus climbed out of the pram.

'Don't go too close to the water, Gus,' warned Mum.

Gus grinned and ran towards the ducks. The ducks scattered, squawking in disgust. Gus jumped in a puddle.

Lulu thought the park seemed very quiet today. Normally there were lots of kids playing and dogs running about. Dogs were allowed off their leads here. Jessie smiled up at Lulu. Jessie and Asha loved Lagoon Park.

Lulu unclipped the leads. Asha and Jessie raced off. They took it in turns to chase each other in mad circles. When they were tired they flopped into the cool water of the lagoon.

'Gussie swim too?' asked Gus.

'Not today, honey bun,' said Mum.
'I think there might be a surprise if we
keep going.' She pushed the pram along
the footpath. The kids followed. Lulu
wondered what the surprise could be.

The family rounded a bend. Lulu
noticed something different about the
park. At the far end there was a large red-
and-white striped tent. A blue-and-gold
pennant fluttered on top. Some caravans
were parked behind the tent too.

'The circus!' called Lulu. 'It's here.'

Mum grinned. 'I told you we might
see something fun if we walked the long
way.'

'Come on, Rosie,' cried Lulu.
'Let's hurry.'

Lulu, Rosie and Gus ran towards the
circus camp. Circus workers hurried back

and forth. Men were securing the ropes and pegs of the big tent. A crowd of people had gathered to watch.

Several temporary yards had been
set out for the animals. Sandy-coloured
camels peered over the fence. They gently
chewed their cud.

Snow-white horses were being
unloaded from the back of a truck.
A woman led them two-by-two down
the ramp. They arched their necks and
tossed their manes.

The woman led the horses into one
of the yards and shut the gate. They
began to graze, their tails swishing.

'I wish we could take them home,'
said Lulu.

There was so much to see. Mum
held Gus's hand so he couldn't get into
mischief. Lulu clipped the two dogs back
on their leads. She didn't want them to
get lost in the milling crowd.

A girl with tangled black hair wandered past. She wore a big, sloppy jumper, shorts and bare feet. She was about ten years old and walking a group of six dogs on leads. Lulu recognised a chocolate Labrador, two black poodles, two tan-and-white terriers and a golden retriever. The dogs yapped and barked.

'Look at the girl with all the dogs,' said Lulu. 'Do you think she is one of the circus performers?'

Rosie shook her head. 'No. She's not wearing a tutu or a tiara.'

Mum laughed. 'She probably wouldn't wear a tiara to walk the dogs. Only when she was performing.'

Rosie twisted a long dark ringlet around her finger. 'I would if I was a circus girl.'

Asha sniffed at a small dog that was wandering past. It was a small, fluffy terrier with a hot-pink handkerchief knotted around its neck. It had a cream body with furry grey ears and a scruffy black face. The dog woofed at Asha and licked her on the nose.

'Hello, gorgeous,' said Lulu. 'Where's your owner?'

The dog woofed again. Then it trotted off after the circus girl.

'Look, Mum,' called Rosie. 'A juggler.' Lulu turned to watch, forgetting the dog.

Rosie pointed to the workmen who
had been erecting the tent. One had
pulled three red balls from his overall
pockets. He tossed and juggled them
in the air. The balls spun in a whirring
circle.

Another workman began turning somersaults. He sprang from hands to feet over and over again. His body spun so fast he was almost a blur. He whizzed around the juggler.

The crowd clapped and cheered.

'Man flying,' said Gus.

'He's an acrobat,' said Mum. 'It must have taken him years to learn how to somersault so well.'

'Wow,' said Lulu. 'I wish I could do that.'

Gus promptly began to try. After one attempt he landed in a tangled heap of boy, boots and cowboy hat. Lulu laughed and helped Gus up. She pulled dried grass out of his hair and dusted off his shirt.

The acrobat sprang back to his feet. He swept a deep bow.

'Come along to see the world-famous Starlight Circus,' called the acrobat. 'Be amazed and enthralled. Be thrilled and intrigued. Roll up, folks. Buy your tickets for the grand opening on Friday night.'

Lulu jiggled with excitement. 'Please can we go, Mum?' she begged.

Mum smiled. 'We'll see how we go, honey buns. But now we need to get home.'

Mum turned to Gus and pointed at the pram seat. 'In you hop, Gus. I think we've had more than enough circus fun for one day.'

Gus climbed into the pram and jammed his cowboy hat on his head. He popped his thumb in his mouth.

'I could never have too much circus fun,' said Lulu. 'I wish we *lived* in a circus!'

# Chapter 3

# The Missing Pup

Rosie and Lulu walked beside the pram. Asha and Jessie trotted along beside them, sniffing all the smells. They came to the end of the park.

'Spangles!' cried a voice. 'Spangles!'

Everyone turned around.

A girl was running towards them. She had tangled black hair, a big, sloppy jumper and bare feet. Her face was streaked with tears.

'Are you all right?' asked Mum.
'Have you hurt yourself?"

The girl shook her head. She wiped
her hand across her cheek. It left a
grubby smear.

'I've . . . lost my dog,' she said.
Her voice cracked. 'Have you seen her?
She's cream and fluffy with a black face.'

'You mean the
cute one with the
pink cloth tied
around her neck?'
asked Lulu.

The girl
nodded. She
looked hopeful.
'Did you see her?
Where was she?'

'We saw you
walking a big group

19

of dogs earlier,' said Lulu. She pointed back towards the circus tent. 'The little dog was following you.'

'She *was*,' said the circus girl. 'But she must have wandered off. I put all the other dogs away in their kennels. When I called Spangles she didn't come.' A tear rolled down her cheek.

'Don't worry.' Mum pulled a tissue out of her handbag and handed it to the circus girl. 'I'm sure Spangles won't be too far away.'

The girl wiped her face and blew her nose.

Lulu tossed her honey-gold ponytail over her shoulder. 'We can help you find Spangles. Can't we, Mum?' asked Lulu.

Mum smiled at the girl. 'Of course we can. Why don't we search back through the park? You girls look down this side. Gus and I will search along the lagoon bank.'

Lulu, Rosie and the girl set off across the grass.

'Hi, I'm Lulu Bell,' Lulu told the circus girl. 'This is my sister Rosie. These are our dogs Asha and Jessie.'

'I'm Stella,' the girl replied. She patted Asha and Jessie.

The girls called and whistled as they walked along. They asked several people if they had seen a small lost dog. No-one had. Lulu glanced towards the lagoon. She could see Mum and Gus walking beside the rushes.

'Do you live in the circus?' asked Rosie.

Stella nodded and pointed back towards the camp. 'I live in the little blue caravan on the end with my mum and dad.'

'Wow. That must be so exciting,' said Lulu.

'It is fun,' agreed Stella. 'We're all trick riders. We also train the dogs. Spangles is my very own dog. I've had her since she was a tiny puppy.' Stella's voice wobbled. 'Mum and Dad are going to be so upset if we can't find Spangles. She is the star of our new act.'

Lulu patted Stella on the shoulder. 'We'll find her,' said Lulu. But the longer they searched, the less certain she felt.

At last they joined up with Mum and Gus at the beach end of the park.

'No luck?' asked Mum.

'No luck at all,' answered Lulu gloomily.

Stella blinked and looked away.

'Doggy *gorn*,' said Gus helpfully. He shrugged his shoulders.

Spangles seemed to have disappeared. Where could the circus pup possibly be?

## Chapter 4

# Still No Luck

'We'll walk back to the camp with you,' said Mum. 'Perhaps we missed Spangles along the way. But then we need to head home. It's getting late.'

Stella nodded. Her eyes darted back and forth. But there was still no sign of the dog. Lulu was getting very worried.

Finally they reached the camp. The workers had finished setting up the big circus tent. Most of them had returned to their caravans to cook dinner.

The crowd of onlookers had gone home too. It was getting dark.

The acrobat who had been turning somersaults walked past. He was carrying buckets of water for the camels. The camels peered over the fence.

'Rory,' called Stella, 'is Spangles back yet?'

Rory shook his head. 'Sorry, Stella. No sign of her. But your mum wants you to go back to the caravan now.'

Stella kicked a clod of earth with her foot. She looked like she might cry again.

'Don't be sad, Stella,' said Rosie.

Asha licked Stella on the hand to comfort her.

'Spangles will probably come home at dinnertime when she gets hungry,' said Mum. 'Our dogs wouldn't miss dinner for anything.'

'Or someone might find her and bring her to our vet hospital,' Lulu told Stella with a smile. 'We live just up the hill at the Shelly Beach Vet Hospital. My dad is the vet there. People often bring lost animals to us.'

Stella cheered up again. 'Thanks so much for your help. I'd better go before Mum gets worried about me.' Stella waved and ran off.

'Bye Stella,' chorused Lulu, Rosie and Gus.

The Bell family waited while Stella ran up the steps of the little blue caravan. With a final wave, she disappeared inside.

'Wouldn't it be fun to live in a caravan?' asked Lulu. 'We could travel all over the countryside with our dogs and horses.'

Lulu's mind filled with exciting images of living in a circus. She would train Asha and Jessie to walk on their hind legs. She would dress in spangled tutus and walk the tightrope. She would stand up on a bareback horse and gallop around the ring. The audience would go wild!

'But I'd miss my friends,' said Rosie. 'And home.'

'Yes, but think of the adventures we'd have!' said Lulu. 'I'd love to be a circus performer.'

# Chapter 5

# The Walk Home

The far end of Lagoon Park was next to a busy road. The family stopped to check for traffic. Cars whizzed past. Lulu held Asha's lead tightly.

'I'd better take Jessie's lead for a while,' Mum said to Rosie. 'There's a lot of traffic along here.'

Rosie handed Mum the lead.

'Let's hope Spangles didn't run onto the road,' said Lulu. 'I'd hate her to be in an accident.'

'We would have heard something if that had happened,' said Mum. 'I'm sure Spangles will be all right.'

Once they had crossed, the girls walked in front. They chatted about the circus. Asha trotted along, her nose twitching. It was almost completely dark now. The cars had switched on their headlights.

There was a short gap in the traffic. In the sudden quiet, Lulu heard a funny noise. A soft, low sound. *What could it be?* Lulu wondered. The faint noise came again.

Asha began to run, her nose to the ground. She strained against the lead. Lulu pulled back, then decided to run with her. Asha bolted into a dark side street.

'Lulu?' called Mum. 'Where *are* you going?'

'We heard something,' Lulu called over her shoulder.

The sound came again. This time Lulu recognised it. A whimper. Somewhere in the darkness a dog was hurt or frightened.

Asha stopped abruptly. She thrust her nose under a thick bush. Lulu crouched down and peered into the shadows.

A car zoomed past. In the sudden glare of its headlights, Lulu saw a dark shape. She could just see a splash of pink cloth.

'Spangles?' asked Lulu. The shadow whined softly. Asha wagged her tail. Lulu slowly held out her hand to the little dog. Dad had always warned her to be careful when approaching injured animals. Sometimes they could bite if they were frightened.

The dry leaves rustled. The shadowy dog was thumping its tail. Lulu stroked the dog's side. It was damp and sticky.

'It's all right, Spangles,' said Lulu in a soothing voice. 'We'll get you home soon.'

Spangles whimpered again.

'Mum, Mum,' called Lulu. Her voice squeaked with excitement. 'We found Spangles.'

Mum, Rosie, Gus and Jessie arrived
just a moment later. Gus scrambled out of
the pram. They crowded around the bush,
straining to see.

Mum ran her hand over the dog
gently. Spangles wagged her tail again.
Asha licked the smaller dog on the face.

'Is she all right?' asked Lulu.

'I think so, but we'll take her home to
make sure,' said Mum. 'Well done, Lulu.
It's so lucky you found her.'

Lulu gave a big grin. She patted Asha on the head.

'It was Asha, really,' said Lulu. 'We heard a whimper. Then Asha followed her scent.'

Mum carefully lifted Spangles out of the leafy hollow. Spangles winced.

'Doggy sore?' asked Gus. He pushed his cowboy hat back on his head.

'Can she walk?' asked Rosie.

'I think we might give her a lift in the pram,' suggested Mum. 'You hop in, Gus. Then you can cuddle Spangles on your lap.'

Gus climbed into the pram. 'Gussie cuddle doggy!' he demanded.

Mum wrapped Spangles in Gus's blanket. She then placed the dog carefully on Gus's lap.

Lulu put her hand on her hip. 'Be gentle with Spangles,' she warned.

Gus grinned at Lulu. 'Gussie like doggy.'

Lulu smiled back. 'I can't wait to see Stella's face when we take Spangles back to her. She will be so excited!'

# Chapter 6

# Surprise!

A few minutes later, they arrived home
at Shelly Beach Veterinary Hospital.
Lulu pushed open the door. The whole
family poured into the waiting room.
Kylie, the vet nurse, was tidying up the
reception desk.

'Hi Kylie,' said Lulu. 'Is Dad here?
We have a patient we need him to check.'

Kylie smiled in welcome. She glanced
at the small dog huddled on Gus's lap.

'He's in his consulting room,' Kylie said. 'His last appointment just left.'

Mum lifted Spangles out of the pram, still wrapped in the blanket. She put her in Lulu's arms.

'You take Spangles to see Dad, honey bun,' suggested Mum. 'I'll head in and cook dinner. If Spangles is all right, you and Dad can take her back to Stella. She'll be so worried about her.'

The rest of the Bell family headed through a thick green door. This door separated their home from the vet hospital in front.

Lulu carried Spangles into the consulting room. Lulu's dad was working on his computer.

'Hello, sweetheart,' said Dad. 'Who do you have there?'

Lulu explained all about the circus and Spangles getting lost and found.

Dad carefully lifted Spangles onto the examination table. Spangles shivered. In the strong light of the consulting room, she looked sad and sorry.

Her grey ears drooped. Her creamy
fur was damp and tangled with leaves.
Her pink neckerchief was muddy.

'Poor little Spangles,' said Dad.

Dad checked her all over thoroughly.
He cleaned the sticky spot on her side
and dabbed on some ointment.

'Is she all right?' Lulu asked anxiously.

'She has a couple of scratches,' said
Dad. 'But I think she's more frightened
than hurt.'

Lulu smiled with relief. 'Can we take
her back to Stella now?'

'Let's go,' said Dad. 'I must admit
I'm keen to meet these circus friends
of yours.'

Dad wrapped Spangles in a clean
towel. He popped her in a cardboard box.
They drove back to Lagoon Park and
walked along the path.

Lulu carried Spangles in the box. The circus camp glowed in the darkness. The big tent was hung with fairy lights. The windows of the caravans gleamed. Delicious cooking smells wafted by.

'Stella lives in the blue caravan at the end,' explained Lulu.

Dad knocked on the caravan door.

Stella opened it. She had a puzzled look on her face. 'Lulu?'

'Surprise!' cried Lulu. She held out the box. 'We have a present for you.'

The present woofed.

'Spangles?' shrieked Stella. 'You found her?'

Stella tore up the lid of the box. Spangles leaped straight into Stella's arms. Stella buried her face in Spangles' fur and rubbed her nose on Spangles' face.

Spangles licked the tears away from
Stella's cheeks.

Stella looked up at Lulu. 'Thank you.
Thank you so much!'

Lulu grinned back. 'It was a pleasure.'

Stella's parents crowded around.
Lulu explained how Spangles had been
found. Dr Bell assured them that she was
perfectly fine.

'Come in and take a seat.' Stella's
mum Jenna waved her hand towards

the neat little table and benches in the middle of the caravan. 'Can I offer you a cup of tea?'

Dr Bell shook his head. 'Thank you. But we had better get home for dinner.'

Lulu gazed longingly into the caravan. She so wanted to go in and have a good look around.

Jenna smiled at her. 'Would you like to come back tomorrow morning, Lulu? Stella would love to show you around. She can introduce you to all the animals.'

Lulu shook her head. She felt so disappointed. 'I have school tomorrow.'

Stella grinned at her. 'Come straight after school.'

Lulu was thrilled. She hopped from one foot to the other. 'Can I, Dad? Pleeeease?'

43

'I don't see why not,' replied Dad. He stroked Lulu's hair away from her forehead. 'My wife Chrissie can drop her over just after three o'clock.'

Lulu hugged Dad tight. 'Thanks, Dad. Thanks, Jenna.'

Everyone said their goodbyes, then Lulu and her dad went home.

That night, Lulu thought she would never get to sleep. How could she ever wait until tomorrow afternoon? How could she ever wait to visit Stella and the circus camp?

## Chapter 7

# After School

Of course, tomorrow afternoon finally came. Mum and Gus picked the girls up from school. They drove to Lagoon Park.

At the circus camp, Lulu recognised Rory the acrobat. He was feeding hay to the camels. Lulu thought one of the camels looked as if she had been eating far too much hay already. She had a big round stomach.

Rory scratched the camel between the eyes. 'Good girl, Goldie.'

The camel stuck her nose in the air.

'Excuse me,' said Lulu. 'Do you know where we can find Stella?'

The acrobat looked over. His eyes twinkled. 'Ah, you must be the girl who found our missing star. Stella's over there.'

Stella was mucking out the horse yard. She had a shovel and was piling horse poo in a wheelbarrow. Spangles was chasing the shovel, darting back and forth.

Stella walked over, wiping her hand

across her forehead. 'You see it's not all *glamour* working in the circus.'

'I thought we'd be doing circus tricks,' joked Lulu.

Stella sprang into a series of cartwheels. Then she swung upside down and walked on her hands. Spangles joined in. She leaped up on her hind legs and walked like a human.

Gus tried to copy Stella. He put both hands on the ground and kicked his legs in the air. He wibbled and wobbled.

His hat fell off. He collapsed on the ground in a tangle. He jumped to his feet and tried again.

Lulu laughed at the sight. Stella swung the right way up. Then she picked up her shovel.

'Can I help you?' asked Lulu. 'I help our vet nurse clean out the animal pens all the time.'

'That would be great. Thanks!' Stella pushed the wheelbarrow over to the fence.

Stella's mum Jenna came over and introduced herself to Lulu's family. Jenna and Mum chatted for a while. Lulu helped Stella unload the wheelbarrow onto the compost pile. Rosie and Gus played with Spangles.

'Well, we'd better get home,' said Mum, at last. 'Shall I come back to get

Lulu at about five o'clock?'

'Could Lulu stay until about seven?' suggested Jenna. 'I thought she might like to have dinner with us in the caravan. Do you like spaghetti bolognaise?'

Lulu beamed. 'I *love* spaghetti bolognaise. Please, Mum, can I stay?'

Mum looked unsure. She glanced at Lulu then at Jenna.

'I promise we'll look after her,' Jenna said. 'It will be so nice for Stella to have a friend over to play. There aren't many other children living in our circus.'

Mum smiled at Jenna. 'Lulu would love to stay for dinner. Okay, we'll see you at seven o'clock.'

Lulu hugged Mum goodbye. Stella swung upside down again. She walked off on her hands, her legs waving in the air.

'Come on,' cried Stella. 'I've so much to show you.'

# Chapter 8

# Circus Fun!

Stella's dad Paul was in the red-and-white striped tent. 'We call it the big top,' explained Stella. The tent was filled with rows of seats. In the middle was a big ring filled with sawdust. Stella and Lulu took a seat in the front row. Spangles plopped down beside them.

In the centre of the ring was Paul. He was training the six dogs. He used arm gestures and voice commands to direct the dogs through their act.

'Hup, Queenie. Hup, Mousse.' Two of the dogs jumped up on their hind legs. They strolled around in a circle. One had a handbag hooked over its front paw. She looked like a lady out shopping.

'Down, girls,' commanded Paul. 'Good job.' He fed them each a titbit from his pocket. Their tails wagged madly.

Spangles jumped over the low wall into the ring. She dashed over to Paul. Spangles sat back and begged. Then she jumped up on her hind legs and pranced around in circles.

'She looks like she's dancing,' said Lulu.

'Spangles is only young but she's very clever,' agreed Stella. 'She loves to perform.'

Paul laughed and gave Spangles a snack. The little dog joined in the performance. Mousse, the chocolate Labrador, trotted into the ring. He was pushing a large silver ball with his nose. The poodle jumped on the ball and ran on top of it.

Another terrier pedalled into the ring on a tricycle. He looked very pleased with himself.

Lulu laughed. 'How did you teach him to do that?'

'Patience and practice,' said Stella. 'Not to mention a pocket full of meaty treats.'

One by one the dogs jumped through a hoop held high by Paul. They ran across a cable, just like tightrope-walkers.

Lastly, the seven dogs lined up in a row. Paul gave a downward signal. The dogs stretched out their front legs. They bobbed their heads to the ground.

'They're bowing,' cried Lulu. She clapped her hands.

Paul turned and swept the girls a graceful bow. The dogs trotted out of the ring, followed by their master.

As soon as the dogs disappeared, six white horses galloped in. The horses had scarlet bridles but no saddles. Jenna ran into the ring after them. She was still dressed in her shabby work clothes. She had a long dressage whip in her hand. She used this to signal to the horses.

'They are liberty horses,' explained Stella. 'They're running free with no leads to guide them. My mother tells them what to do.'

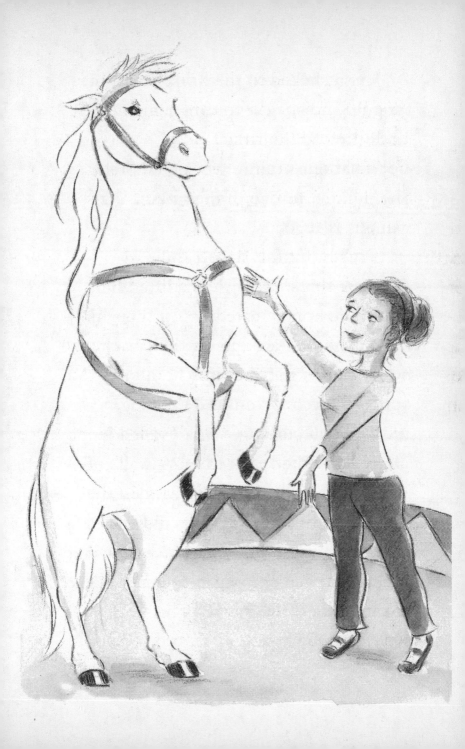

Jenna clicked to the horses with her tongue. They began to canter in an even circle around the ring.

'That one's mine,' whispered Stella. She pointed to one of the horses. 'His name is Blanco.'

'He's beautiful,' sighed Lulu.

After three circles, Jenna lifted her arms. The horses reared up on their hind legs. They spun around on their back hooves. Then they began to canter in the opposite direction around the ring.

'Are you coming, Stella?' called Jenna.

Stella vaulted over the low wall and into the ring. She dodged between the cantering horses. The horses didn't miss a beat. Stella stood in the centre of the ring watching. Then she began to run straight towards one of the horses. This horse was wearing a thick pad on his broad back.

Lulu gasped. What was Stella doing?

Stella ran beside Blanco then swung up onto his back. She cantered along for a few moments. Then she leaped to her feet with her right foot forward. She stood up tall with her back straight and her head high. The horse continued its steady even gait. Stella waved to Lulu and grinned.

'That's amazing,' called Lulu. 'Aren't you scared you'll fall?'

Stella didn't answer. Instead she raised one leg behind her and pointed her toe. Lulu forgot Stella's shabby clothes and bare feet. She looked like a graceful ballerina. A ballerina dancing on top of a cantering horse! Stella jumped and landed safely again on the horse's back. She turned around and faced backwards.

'Woohoo,' called Stella. She waved to Lulu.

Stella leaped to the ground again.
She ran to Lulu and curtseyed.

Lulu clapped her hands together.
'That was wonderful,' she cried. 'I wish
I could do that.'

'It's nothing special,' Stella said
modestly. 'I learned to do that years ago.'

'Don't you slip off?' asked Lulu.

'The pad on Blanco's back is rubbed
with rosin to make it sticky,' explained
Stella. 'I bet I could teach you how to do
some circus tricks.'

Lulu swallowed. 'Really?'

Stella swung over to walk on her
hands. She waggled her feet at Lulu.
'It takes hard work and lots of practice.
But really it's all about good balance.'

Lulu flicked one of her honey-
coloured plaits over her shoulder.
'Could you show me?'

Stella grinned. 'I'd love to.'

'What would you like to learn?' asked Stella. 'I can teach you to juggle, walk on your hands, do cartwheels or some horseback tricks.'

'I learned to do cartwheels and handstands at gymnastics,' replied Lulu. She showed Stella a quick series of spinning cartwheels. 'But I'd love to learn how to walk on my hands. And some horseback tricks! Do you think you could teach me to stand up on a horse's back?'

'Can you ride?' asked Stella.

'I love riding. I've had lessons and I often ride at my uncle's farm,' replied Lulu.

Stella nodded. 'Let's get to work,' she said.

Lulu and Stella worked together for the rest of the afternoon. It didn't take Lulu long to learn to walk a little way on her hands. Spangles trotted along beside her on her hind legs.

Then Stella's mum Jenna offered to teach Lulu some horseriding tricks. She put a saddle with special straps on Blanco. Lulu put on a helmet.

She rode Blanco slowly around the ring. Blanco was so well trained that he was very easy to ride. Jenna soon had Lulu trotting, then cantering in big circles around the ring.

'Now, let's try something a bit harder,' suggested Jenna.

Lulu's heart beat fast with excitement. 'Yes, please.'

# Chapter 9

# Goldie in Trouble

When Lulu arrived home she was full of stories about her afternoon at the circus.

'Stella and her mum have asked me to come back again tomorrow,' said Lulu. 'I can go, can't I, Mum? And I'm going to teach Asha and Jessie how to walk on their hind legs. And Stella said I can come back on Friday before opening night.'

Mum laughed. 'You certainly have had an adventure, haven't you, Lulu?

I think you can visit again tomorrow.'

Lulu threw herself at Mum and hugged her tight. 'Thanks! You're the best mum in the world.'

Later that night, Lulu changed into her pyjamas. She came out to kiss Mum and Dad goodnight. Before she could, the vet hospital phone rang. At night, the phone rang through to the house for emergencies.

Dad answered. 'Dr Bell speaking.' He listened while the other person spoke. 'Okay. I'm on my way.'

Dad turned to Mum and Lulu. 'That was the circus. Apparently they have a camel who needs some help. I said I'd go straight away.'

Lulu looked up at her Dad. 'Can I come too? *Pleeease*, Dad.'

'It's a school night,' Mum reminded her.

Dad grinned. 'We won't be long.
And it's not often we get a house call to
a circus to treat a camel!'

Mum smiled. 'Okay, but don't be late.'

Lulu pulled a hoodie over her
pyjamas. Dad grabbed
his black medical bag.
In a few minutes they
were back at the circus.

A small throng of people stood beside the camel enclosure. There was Rory the acrobat, Percy the juggler, Stella, Jenna and Paul. They were all holding torches. Rory looked worried.

One of the camels was lying down in the straw. Lulu thought she looked very uncomfortable with her big round stomach. The camel was breathing heavily. She let out an indignant roar.

'It's Goldie,' said Rory. 'She's having a baby. But she seems to be in trouble.'

Dad knelt down in the straw. He poked and prodded the camel's bulging belly. He smiled. 'Goldie will be fine. She just needs a little help. But I don't think she's having a baby . . . I think she's having twins!'

Rory grinned with relief. Lulu gave Stella a hug. Twin baby camels!

'We need to give her a little peace and space,' suggested Dad. 'Rory, could you please hold the torch for me? Everyone else, just step back a little.'

Dad set to work. Soon there were not one but two newborn camels lying in the straw. Dad wiped their noses free of gunk to help them breathe. The firstborn baby struggled to its feet. It was wonky and wobbly on long skinny legs. Its mother licked its nose.

'Two perfect baby girls,' announced Dad. 'Mother and babies in excellent health.'

Paul came up and shook Dad's hand. 'That's the second time in two nights that Lulu's family has helped us. The Starlight Circus would like to thank you very much . . .'

He pulled a sheaf of paper from his pocket. '. . . with front row VIP tickets to Friday's opening night.'

'Hurray!' said Lulu. 'Thank you so much.'

Stella winked at Lulu. Lulu winked right back.

Dad took the tickets. 'We would love to come. Thank you. Now, I promised Chrissie we wouldn't be long. Before we go, have you thought of names for your two new circus performers?'

Rory glanced lovingly at the newborn babies. He scrunched up his face and rubbed his chin. 'Such cute girls deserve two special names. I will call them . . . Stella and Lulu.'

Lulu and Stella exchanged delighted glances.

'Come and see the baby camels again tomorrow?' asked Stella.

'Absolutely!' Lulu gave a super-big grin. What a thrilling night. She couldn't wait to tell her best friend Molly all about it at school.

# Chapter 10

# Opening Night

At last it was Friday night. The opening night of Starlight Circus. Lagoon Park was festooned with twinkling lights. The reflections shimmered and glimmered on the water of the lagoon.

Crowds of people stood around laughing and chatting. Molly was there with her mum Tien and little brother Sam. Jessica was there with her twin brothers Jack and Toby and their parents.

Kylie the vet nurse was there with friends. Everyone waved and called hello.

Dad bought a big box of buttery popcorn. Lulu was so excited she couldn't eat a thing. Gus was very happy to eat her share. Rosie and Lulu had dressed up. Rosie wore a pale-blue tutu, angel wings and a tiara in her hair. Lulu wore a big coat. She had brushed and brushed her hair until it shone.

Lulu jiggled up and down. Finally it was time to take their seats. They had five seats right in the middle of the front row. Lulu wriggled back in her seat.

'Do you want me to take your coat, honey bun?' Mum asked Lulu.

'No thanks, Mum,' said Lulu. 'It's a bit cold.' Mum looked puzzled but didn't argue.

A drum roll sounded. The spotlight shone. Everyone stopped talking.

Into the middle of the ring strode
Stella's dad Paul. He was no longer
dressed in grubby jeans and a stained
T-shirt. He wore snow-white jodhpurs
with long black boots. He had a scarlet
riding jacket and a black top hat. He
looked magnificent.

Paul cracked his whip. 'I am Paulo
Steffiano, the ringmaster. Welcome to the
world-famous Starlight Circus. Tonight
we will dazzle and delight you. Intrigue
and amaze you. Be prepared for the best
night of your lives . . .'

The music began. A horde of acrobats
leaped into the ring. Somersaulting,
spinning, tumbling and turning. Rory
waved to Lulu as he hurtled past.

Clowns with big red noses played
silly games. They fought and made rude
noises. They chased each other and fell

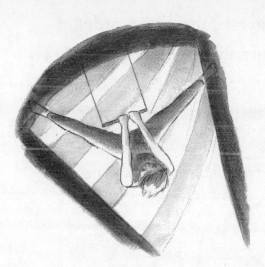

over their
super-long
shoes. The
crowd roared
with laughter.

Aerialists
swung on giant
swings high
above the ring.
They leaped and plummeted and soared
through the air. Lulu held her breath
until they were all safely landed in the
bouncy safety net.

Paul returned to the ring. He tipped
his glossy black hat and gave a flourishing
bow. Six dogs proudly trotted in. They
wore ruffs and tutus. They performed
perfectly – walking on their hind legs,
balancing on a ball, pedalling the tricycle
and walking the tightrope.

The dogs bowed and trotted out. Lulu clapped until her palms were aching.

But where was Spangles?

The clowns returned, pushing and shoving. One had a curly blue wig. He juggled flaming torches. The fire spun up and over in the air.

Another clown was jealous. He ran off and came back wearing a very tall top hat and a huge red coat. He carried a chair and a long whip. He cracked the whip and flourished the chair. He was pretending to be Paulo the ringmaster.

Then came a surprise. A golden lion cub rushed into the ring. The cub growled. It darted back and forth.

The fake ringmaster tried to tame the lion. He cracked his whip. He thrust his chair. He even tried a flaming torch. But the cub was not to be tamed.

Lulu looked closely. She laughed. It wasn't a lion cub at all. It was Spangles dressed up in a furry golden lion suit.

Spangles leaped at the lion tamer clown. The clown threw his chair away and ran. Spangles chased the clown around and around the ring. With a big jump, Spangles lunged for the clown's bottom. The back flap of the clown's trousers fell down. Underneath were pink polka dot undies. The clown fell on his back. Spangles leaped on his chest. She licked him all over his face. The crowd laughed even harder.

Spangles rose up on her back legs. She danced pirouettes around the fallen clown. Then she swept a deep bow and raced out of the ring.

The clowns shambled out, shaking their heads and rubbing their bottoms. The applause was deafening.

Spangles was a hit. Whatever could come next?

## Chapter 11

# The Star of the Show

A trumpet tooted. The spotlight shone. Paul strode into the centre of the ring. The crowd went as quiet as the night.

'And now for our next act,' boomed Paul, 'we need a volunteer from the audience. Would anyone like to help us?'

Dozens of hands shot into the air. Lulu stretched her hand as high as she could reach. The ringmaster looked around.

'You. The young lady in the front row.' He pointed straight at Lulu. 'Come on into the ring.'

'Oh, honey bun,' said Mum. 'He means you.'

'Go on, sweetheart,' said Dad.

Lulu took off her coat. She scrambled over the low wall and into the ring. She was wearing black leggings, ballet slippers and a black leotard.

'Are you ready, Lulu?' Paul whispered to her. She nodded. Her mouth felt dry. Paul turned to the audience. 'May I present Miss Lulu Bell of Shelly Beach Vet Hospital.'

The crowd clapped. Dad and Gus stood up and cheered. Lulu waved.

Jenna and Stella came out into the ring. They were both dressed as Spanish flamenco dancers. They wore tight-fitting black dresses. Red and gold ruffles frothed at the shoulders and hem. Spangles followed them.

Jenna carried a matching flamenco skirt. She fastened it around Lulu's waist.

Stella clipped a set of ruffles to her leotard to form sleeves. Now Lulu was dressed as a flamenco dancer too. Both girls put on helmets disguised as Spanish hats.

Jenna whistled. Suddenly six snow-white horses appeared. They cantered in a circle, round and round. All wore scarlet bridles. One of the horses wore a special

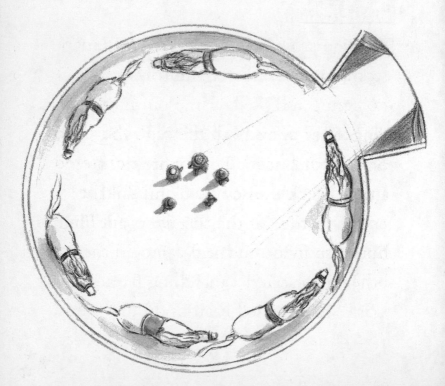

saddle on his back. After two laps, they spun around and cantered the opposite way. Jenna gestured.

The saddled horse stopped. It was Blanco. He walked into the centre, arching his neck. His mane and tail flowed like foaming white water. Blanco lay down on the ground. Lulu climbed onto his back.

Blanco stood and pawed the ground. Lulu waved to the crowd. Then Blanco rejoined the circle of cantering white horses.

Stella ran and vaulted onto the back of another horse. The two girls cantered around. Jenna raised her arms. All the horses reared. Lulu clung on tight. The horses spun around and cantered the other way.

Jenna signalled with her whip. Four of the horses trotted out of the ring. Now there were just two horses, with the girls on their backs. The horses moved slowly and rhythmically in perfect time.

A drum roll sounded. Stella leaped to her feet. She stood on horseback and waved to the crowd.

The crowd roared. Lulu glanced at Jenna. Jenna smiled encouragingly then she signalled with her dressage whip to Blanco.

Lulu grabbed the special strap attached to Blanco's saddle. She held tight and pulled herself to a crouch. Then she stood up. Lulu stood tall and proud as Blanco circled the ring.

The crowd went wild. Lulu gave a super-huge grin. She felt like she was flying! As she rode past she could see

her family and friends. Dad leaped to his
feet. Gus was standing on his chair. Rosie
was waving. Molly clapped and cheered.
Mum had her hand to her mouth.
She looked terrified.

Jenna waved her arms. The girls sat
down again. The horses trotted to the
centre and stopped side by side.

The horses stretched their front legs out and bowed. Their noses dipped to the sawdust. Their tails swished.

The ringmaster called out, 'A huge round of applause for our very own Stella. And for Lulu Bell in her first ever circus performance!'

The crowd applauded. It sounded like thunder. Lulu the circus girl waved and waved. This was a night she would never ever forget. What a magnificent circus adventure.

# Lulu Bell and the Sea Turtle

Lulu and her family are setting off on an adventure a long way from home. Mum has been invited to visit an Aboriginal community to choose paintings for an art show.

Lulu, Rosie and Gus have lots of fun swimming and fishing with their new friends. But there is one thing Lulu would really like to see. Can wishing upon a star help her dream come true?

**Out now**

# Read all the Lulu Bell books

*Lulu Bell and the Birthday Unicorn*

*Lulu Bell and the Fairy Penguin*

*Lulu Bell and the Cubby Fort*

*Lulu Bell and the Moon Dragon*

*Lulu Bell and the Circus Pup*

*Lulu Bell and the Sea Turtle*

*Lulu Bell and the Tiger Cub*

June 2014

*Lulu Bell and the Pyjama Party*

June 2014

# About the Author

Belinda Murrell grew up in a vet hospital and Lulu Bell is based on some of the adventures she shared with her own animals. After studying Literature at Macquarie University, Belinda worked as a travel journalist, editor and technical writer.
A few years ago, she began to write stories for her own three children – Nick, Emily and Lachlan. Belinda's books include the Sun Sword fantasy trilogy, timeslip tales *The Locket of Dreams, The Ruby Talisman* and *The Ivory Rose*, and Australian historical tales *The Forgotten Pearl* and *The River Charm*.

**www.belindamurrell.com.au**

# About the Illustrator

Serena Geddes spent six years working with a fabulously mad group of talented artists at Walt Disney Studios in Sydney before embarking on the path of picture book illustration in 2009. She works both traditionally and digitally and has illustrated many books, ranging from picture books to board books to junior novels.

**www.serenageddes.com.au**